WHO YOU CALLIN' EXTINCT?

The Coolest Joke Book Ever!

™ & © 2002 Twentieth Century Fox Film Corporation. All rights reserved. Printed in the United States of America. No part of this book may be used or reproduced in any manner whatsoever without written permission of the publisher except in the case of brief quotations embodied in critical articles and reviews. For information address HarperCollins Publishers Inc., 10 East 53rd Street, New York, NY 10022.

HarperCollins books are available at special quantity discounts for bulk purchases for sales promotions, premiums, or fund-raising. For information please call or write: Special Markets Department, HarperCollins Publishers Inc., 10 East 53rd Street, New York, NY 10022. Telephone: (212) 207-7528. Fax: (212) 207-7222.

ISBN 0-06-093813-7

HarperCollins®, ☰®, and HarperEntertainment™ are trademarks of HarperCollins Publishers Inc.

First printing: February 2002

Visit HarperEntertainment on the World Wide Web at www.harpercollins.com

10 9 8 7 6 5 4 3 2 1

WHO YOU CALLIN' EXTINCT?

The Coolest Joke Book Ever!

BY JUDY KATSCHKE

HarperEntertainment

An Imprint of HarperCollinsPublishers

So you think the Ice Age is history? Well, guess what? Your uncle Bob's hairy back is no accident. Trust me. The Ice Age can come blowing our way in just another 70,000 years or so. But before you get your winter woollies in a twist, here are a few ways to know if the Ice Age is coming to your town.

1. Your school bus is being pulled by a team of huskies!
2. Your long underwear is never long enough!
3. That clicking sound isn't your keyboard—it's your teeth!
4. The only thing hot in the school cafeteria is the taco sauce!
5. Brr! Brr! You're growing fur!

But if you take my advice, there are loads of ways to kill the chill. Just think warm, fuzzy thoughts.

Or you could try some of these gags and groaners on your friends. Every one of them has survived at least 10,000 years.

SURVIVAL RATE OF AN ICE AGE JOKE: 10,000 YEARS.

SURVIVAL RATE OF A SCRAT: 2 MINUTES.

WHAT'S WRONG WITH THIS PICTURE?

CARL: What will the forest
say when this Ice Age is
finally over?
FRANK: What?
CARL: What a re-leaf!

DIEGO: Knock, knock!
SID: Who's there?
DIEGO: Ada.
SID: Ada who?
DIEGO: Ada nice
juicy sloth
for lunch!

MY, WHAT
BIG TEETH
YOU HAVE!

WAAA!

SID: I have the perfect Ice
   Age story for widdle
   baby-kins!

ROSHAN: Goo goo! (*GURGLE,
   GURGLE.*)

SID: It's called
   "Coldielocks and the
   Three Brrrrrs"!

**HEH,
HEH,
HEH.**

DODO: Dr. Dodo!
   Dr. Dodo! My wife
   thinks she's a pack
   of cards!

DR. DODO: I'll deal with
   her later!

SID: What did the human say when he invented fire?

MANNY: What?

SID: Pass the marshmallows!

MANNY: (*GROAN.*)

SID: Hey, big guy. What do you get when you feed hot cocoa to a snowman?

MANNY: A puddle!

DIEGO: What has four legs and an arm?

SID: Do tell, Diego! Do tell!

DIEGO: A happy tiger!

GULP

MANNY: Watch out, Sid. I was once the
   meanest mammoth in the schoolyard.
SID: Oh, I get it. A real woolly bully!

GRRRRRRR!!

ZEKE: Hey, Oscar. How did
Soto get to be head
saber-toothed honcho?
OSCAR: I guess he clawed his
way to the top!

SID: Diego, my man, as a symbol of our
friendship, please accept this bouquet
of your favorite flowers.
DIEGO: Favorite flowers?
What are my
favorite flowers?
SID: TIGER lilies!
Ha, ha, ha!
DIEGO: (*SNARL!*)

OSCAR: Here's some food for thought. What's a saber-toothed tiger's favorite meal?

LENNY: That's easy—baked beings!

MAYBE I SHOULD'VE GOTTEN ... CHOCOLATES?

MANNY: What do you call a crazy snow flurry?

SID: A flake?

MANNY: Hmm. I guess it takes one to know one.

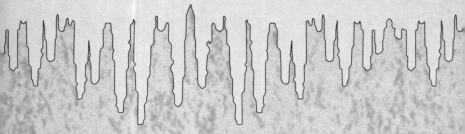

DIEGO: Knock, Knock!
LENNY: Who's there?
DIEGO: Diego!
LENNY: Diego who?
DIEGO: Dee-AY-go before the B!

A, B, C, D. OH, I GET IT!

ZEKE: I'm glad I'm not a
leopard. They can never
escape those hunters.
LENNY: Yeah. They're
always being
spotted!

WHAT A
GENIUS!

MANNY: When this Ice Age
is over, I'm going for
a nice swim.

SID: I wouldn't if I were
you, Manny.

MANNY: Why not?

SID: Because you mammoths
can never keep your
trunks up!

SID: What time is it when
a bunch of woolly
mammoths sit on a
fence?

MANNY: Time to get
another fence!

SID: Oh, HERD that one
already?

CARL: I know a rhino who thinks he's an owl.
FRANK: Who?
CARL: Make that TWO rhinos.

MANNY: Oh, great! Here come the rhinos!

SID: Don't worry, Manny. I know how to keep rhinos from charging.

MANNY: You do? How?

SID: Take away their credit cards!

SID: Manny, Manny! Something
  terrible just happened.
  I lost my memory!
MANNY: When did it happen?
SID: When did WHAT happen?
MANNY: Never
  mind.

SID: Manny, I'll bet this
  baby's favorite game
  is basketball.
MANNY: Basketball?
  What makes
  you say that?
SID: Because he
  loves to dribble!

HUMANS
ARE SO
DISGUSTING.

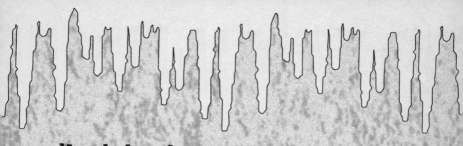

SID: Knock, knock.

SYLVIA: Who's there?

SID: Little old lady.

SYLVIA: Little old lady who?

SID: Sylvia! I didn't know
you could yodel!

OH, SID, YOU'RE SUCH A HOOT.

MANNY: Yo, Sid. What's black and white and red all over?

SID: I don't know, Manny!

MANNY: A penguin with a sunburn.

SID: Ow!

MANNY: What's black and white and blue all over?

SID: What?

MANNY: A penguin with frostbite!

SID: I'm glad I'm not a penguin, Manny.

MANNY: Me, too, Sid.

DOOM ON YOU.

SID: **Manny, Manny! It's those dodo birds again. They think they're a bridge!**

MANNY: **A bridge? What's come over them?**

SID: **A herd of rhinos, a dozen humans, and some migrating aardvarks.**

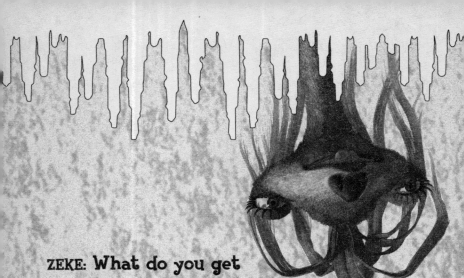

ZEKE: What do you get
  when you cross a
  snowman with a
  saber-toothed tiger?
LENNY: Frostbite!

SYLVIA: Knock, knock.
SID: Who's there?
SYLVIA: Aardvark.
SID: Aardvark who?
SYLVIA: Aardvark a million
  miles for one of your
  smiles.
SID: I was afraid of that!

A group of tigers walked into a restaurant. "Do you serve dodos here?" Soto asked. "We serve anybody!" the waiter said. "Have a seat!"

VERY FUNNY, SYLVIA.

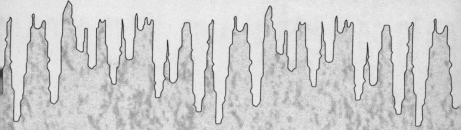

SID: Those rhinos must be awesome musicians!

MANNY: Why, Sid?

SID: Because they never leave without their horns!

MANNY: I wonder what humans do for fun in the Ice Age?

SID: I'll bet they like to dance.

MANNY: Why do you say that?

SID: Because there are plenty of snowballs!

SID: Manny, everyone thinks
I'm a liar.

MANNY: I don't believe you.

SID: Everyone keeps
disagreeing with me!

MANNY: No, they don't.

SID: And nobody takes me
seriously anymore!

MANNY: You must be joking.

SID: (*SIGH.*) Why do I
bother?

LENNY: What do you call
a tropical bird
in the Ice Age?

ZEKE: What?

LENNY: Lost!

ONE WAY

27

SOTO: **How do you make a rhino float?**

DIEGO: **How?**

SOTO: **Add milk and ice cream!**

DIEGO: **My mouth is watering already!**

SID: **Why did the dodo cross the road?**

MANNY: **Why?**

SID: **Because chickens haven't evolved yet!**

MANNY: **That's a real yuk.**

SID: **More like a cluck!**

CLUCK YUK YUK!

DODO #1: Knock, knock.

DODO #2: Who's there?

DODO #1: Shelby.

DODO #2: Shelby who?

DODO #1: Shelby comin' round the mountain when she comes! Shelby comin' round the mountain when she comes!

SID: Hey, Manny, what do you do when a woolly mammoth sneezes?

MANNY: What?

SID: Open an umbrella . . .

MANNY: Ah . . . ah . . . ah—

SID: And run for cover!

YEE-HAA!

SID: Hey, big guy. I know
something that's the
same size as you but
doesn't weigh a thing.
MANNY: Impossible. What?
SID: Your shadow!

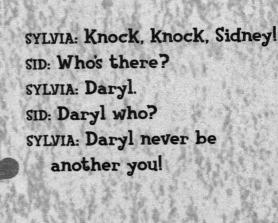

SYLVIA: Knock, knock, Sidney!
SID: Who's there?
SYLVIA: Daryl.
SID: Daryl who?
SYLVIA: Daryl never be
another you!

SID: Excuse me, operator, but what's the best way to call a saber-toothed tiger?

OPERATOR: Long distance!

SID: Good idea.

UM, EASY ON THE MUSH, SYLVIA.

MANNY: Knock, knock!

SID: Who's there?

MANNY: Harry.

SID: Harry who?

MANNY: Harry up and get this baby home!

MANNY: OKay, wise guy, what do you get when you cross a sloth with a dinosaur?

SID: What?

DIEGO: Lazy bones!

SID: What do you get when you cross a tiger with a tortoise?

MANNY: What?

SID: A striped turtleneck!

SID: What do you get when you cross a mammoth with a Kangaroo?

MANNY: What?

SID: A woolly jumper!

OY!

OSCAR: Hey, Soto, where's
the best place to keep
money in the Ice Age?

SOTO: Where?

OSCAR: In a snowbank!

SOTO: Cheap joke.

SID: Manny, we'd better
knit this baby another
sock!

MANNY: Why?

SID: Just in case he grows
another foot!

SID: Knock, knock.

MANNY: Who's there?

SID: Cargo.

MANNY: Cargo who?

SID: Car goes BEEP,
BEEP, BEEP!

I CRACK
MYSELF
UP!

MANNY: I just had the worst vacation.

SID: No kidding, Manny. How come?

MANNY: The hotel lost my trunk!

SID: Bummer.

CARL: Knock, knock.

FRANK: Who's there?

CARL: Lettuce.

FRANK: Lettuce who?

CARL: Lettuce in and we'll tell you!

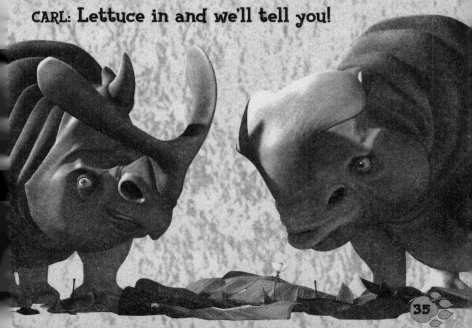

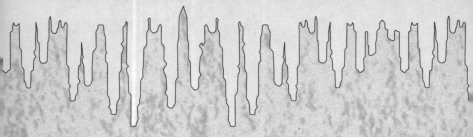

DIEGO: Knock, knock.

SID: Who's there?

DIEGO: Howard.

SID: Howard who?

DIEGO: Howard you like half of my sloth-burger?

I DON'T THINK SO.

DIEGO: What kind of cat should you NEVER play cards with?

SID: I don't know. What kind?

DIEGO: A cheat-ah!

SID: Ha, ha! Ya killin' me, Diego! Ya killin' me!

DIEGO: Don't . . . give . . . me . . . any . . . ideas.

DODO #1: Where does a wolf
　　　sit at a campfire?
DODO #2: Anywhere he
　　　wants!
DODO #1: That's a howl!

SID: Hey, Manny. Did you
hear the joke about
the jump rope?
MANNY: No. Let's just
skip it.

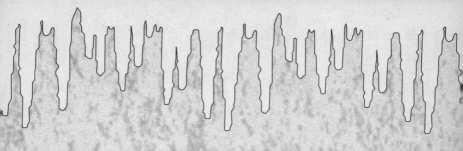

HEEEELP!

SYLVIA: Knock, knock.

SID: Who's there?

SYLVIA: Justin.

SID: Justin who?

SYLVIA: Justin time to
give you a kiss!

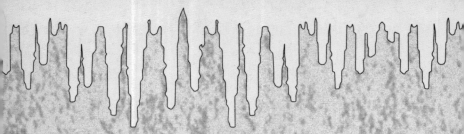

MANNY: What's faster—heat or cold?

SID: Cold!

MANNY: Nope. Heat.

SID: Why?

MANNY: Because you can catch a cold!

I CAN'T BELIEVE I FELL FOR THAT OLD JOKE.

SOTO: Bring me something to eat. And make it snappy!

LENNY: How about a crocodile?

MANNY: Hey, Sid, what do you call a tiger wearing earmuffs?

SID: Anything you want. He can't hear us, anyway!

SID: Manny! Manny! A wolf just bit off my arm. What do I do?

MANNY: Go to a second-hand shop!

SID: Manny! Manny! A wolf just bit off my foot. What do I do?

MANNY: Call a toe truck!

THAT'S HILARIOUS ...NOT.

SID: Whew! I just got charged by a herd of rhinos!

SYLVIA: Oh, no, Sid—what did you do?

SID: What else? I paid them!

DIEGO: What goes in the water pink and comes out blue?

SOTO: What?

DIEGO: A human swimmer in the Ice Age!

SOTO: Mmm. Where can I find one?

DIEGO: Try the frozen-food section!

HA! HA! HA!

LENNY: Hey, Diego, how do you like your burger?

DIEGO: Medium roarrrrr!

LENNY: What would you like to drink with that?

DIEGO: How about a handshake?

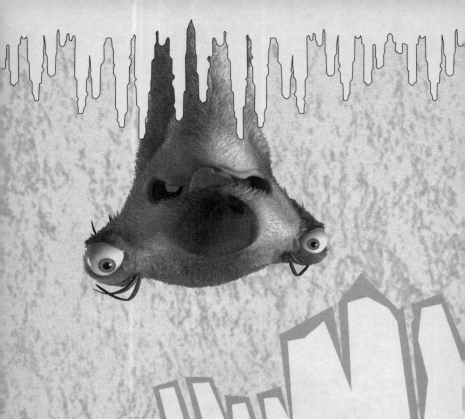

SID: Hey, Sylvia. How did rhinos get such sharp horns?

SYLVIA: By standing too close to the pencil sharpener!

SID: Hmm. I get your point!

SID: What did the dodo egg
     say to the blender?
MANNY: I know when I'm beaten.
SID: You crack me up, Manny.

LENNY: Zeke! Zeke! I just
       ate a comedian.
ZEKE: A comedian? How do
       you feel?
LENNY: Funny.

SID: Tell me, Manny. Why do
mammoths like you have
trunks?

MANNY: Because we'd look
pretty stupid with
backpacks!

SID: What do you call a
mammoth hitchhiker?

MANNY: A two-and-a-half-
ton pickup.

SID: You said it—not I!

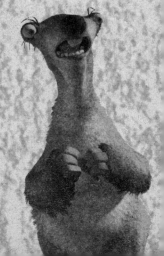

SID: **Knock, knock.**

MANNY: **Who's there?**

SID: **Pitcher.**

MANNY: **Pitcher who?**

SID: (*SINGS*) **Pitcher right foot in, pitcher right foot out, pitcher right foot in and shake it all about!**

AREN'T SLOTHS EXTINCT YET?

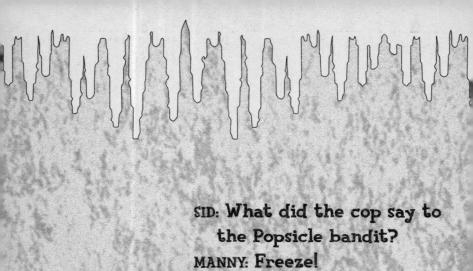

SID: **What did the cop say to the Popsicle bandit?**
MANNY: **Freeze!**

OH, YOU HEARD THAT ONE ALREADY?

OSCAR: How is the Ice Age different from a prizefighter?

DIEGO: One is cold out, the other is out cold!

SID: Guess what, Manny? I just saw a snowman on top of a volcano.

MANNY: Frosty the Snowman?

SID: More like . . . Frosty the BLOWMAN.

LENNY: Oscar, Oscar! I just swallowed a whole bird.

OSCAR: Don't worry. It's tweetable!

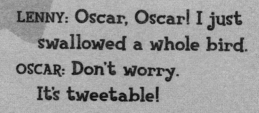

AND NOW, FOR MY BEST JOKE EVER . . .

ZEKE: Knock, knock.

SOTO: Who's there?

ZEKE: Noah.

SOTO: Noah who?

ZEKE: Noah good place to find some humans?

DODO #1: Why is six afraid of seven?

DODO #2: Because seven eight nine!

HA! HA! HA!

SID: Manny! You just sat on a box of animal crackers! What do you have to say for yourself?

MANNY: That's the way the cookie crumbles!

DODO #1: What did the stamp say to the envelope?

DODO #2: What?

DODO #1: Stick with me and we'll go places!

OSCAR: What do you call a bunch of mammoths on roller skates?

LENNY: Mmm. Meals on wheels!

CARL: Frank! You just sat in a field of poison ivy and four-leaf clovers!

FRANK: I know. And I'd do it again.

CARL: Why?

FRANK: Because I need a rash of good luck!

SID: **What do you get when you cross a baby with a scary monster?**

ROSHAN: Goo?

SID: **A creepy crawler!**

ROSHAN: Waaaa!

NOTHING PERSONAL, KID

SYLVIA: Sidney, do you love me?

SID: Of course I do, Sylvia.

SYLVIA: Good. Then whisper something soft and sweet into my ear.

SID: Marshmallow!

Sid and Manny walked into a French restaurant. "Excuse me, waiter," Sid said. "Do you have frog legs?" "No," the waiter replied. "I always walk like this!"

SID: Hey, Manny, would you say I'm a good friend?

MANNY: As friends go, you're okay. And the farther you go, the better!

SID: (SIGH..) Sorry I asked!

SID: Say, Manny, where do saber-toothed tigers like to hang out?

MANNY: Beats me. Where?

SID: At the maul, of course!

SOTO: Lenny, don't you want to chase that charging rhinoceros?

LENNY: Nah. I don't like fast food.

SID: Sylvia! Sylvia! A big old
volcano just erupted!
SYLVIA: Really? How lava-ly!

DODO #1: What's the one ball
that doesn't bounce?
DODO #2: A snowball!

I PREFER
SLOTH
SOUP

SID: Knock, knock!

SYLVIA: Who's there?

SID: Sid!

SYLVIA: Sid who?

SID: Sid down! You're rocking the iceberg!

SYLVIA: Okay! Okay!

I'M STILL NOT LAUGHING. TRY HARDER.

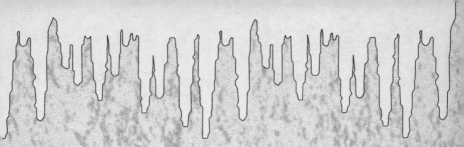

OSCAR: Knock, knock.

SOTO: Who's there?

OSCAR: Oscar.

SOTO: Oscar who?

OSCAR: Oscar if she wants
another serving of rhino!

CARL: What do you get when
you cross a wolf with a
woolen mitten?

FRANK: I don't know. But I'm
not shaking hands with it!

SID: Manny! Manny! Roshan
is floating on a glacier!

MANNY: Oh, no! What's he
doing?

SID: Just going with the floe!

SID: What's a saber-toothed
tiger's favorite day of the
week?

MANNY: I give up.

SID: CHEWS-day!

RIGHT ON!

And last but not least . . .

SID: **Why are Ice Age mammals the best mammals ever?**

MANNY: **Why?**

SID: **Because we're so cool!**

Manfred here. Okay, so I don't have peanut breath. But it's still easy to mistake a big lug like me for an elephant. Especially when ol' Jumbo and I might just be distant cousins. So here are a few things that mammoths and elephants have in common, besides our big butts. . . .

Elephants and mammoths . . .

1. Always wear trunks to the swimming hole.
2. Walk wall-to-wall down the hall.
3. Get regular visits from the tusk fairy.
4. Love the game of squash!

What did I tell ya? There's just one small difference. Jumbo works for peanuts. I prefer cold cash. Hey, call it an Ice Age thing!

Think the Ice Age was too cool for cats? Here are some books you can really sink your saber-tooth into. . . .

MY LIFE IN THE ICE AGE
    by I. C. Cold
IT STINKS TO BE EXTINCT!
    by Ima Gonner
RAISE THE FROZEN MAMMOTH
    by Justin Casey Thaws
AVALANCHE! AVALANCHE! by Danielle Soloud
VOLCANOES THAT LAVA TOO MUCH by I. M. Burned
100 WAYS TO DIAPER A HUMAN BABY by Dee Sposable
THE BIG MELTDOWN by Constant Dripping
INTO THE TIGER'S CAVE by Hugo First
THE MIGHTY MAMMAL MIGRATION by Miles Apart
THE ICE AGE IS COMING! THE ICE AGE IS COMING!
    by Sue Nora Later